YEARLING BOOKS

Since 1966, Yearling has been the

leading name in classic and award-winning

literature for young readers.

With a wide variety of titles,

Yearling paperbacks entertain, inspire,

and encourage a love of reading.

VISIT

WWW.RANDOMHOUSE.COM/KIDS

**TO FIND THE PERFECT BOOK, PLAY GAMES,
AND MEET FAVORITE AUTHORS!**

OTHER YEARLING BOOKS YOU WILL ENJOY

RUNT, *Marion Dane Bauer*

SONG OF SAMPO LAKE, *William Durbin*

SPRING-HEELED JACK, *Philip Pullman*

WHEN MY NAME WAS KEOKO, *Linda Sue Park*

THE FAIRY REBEL, *Lynne Reid Banks*

THERE'S A BOY IN THE GIRLS' BATHROOM
Louis Sachar

TROUT AND ME, *Susan Shreve*

EARTHBORN, *Sylvia Waugh*

SPACE RACE, *Sylvia Waugh*

TADPOLE, *Ruth White*

MY FATHER'S DRAGON

RUTH STILES GANNETT

Illustrated by

RUTH CHRISMAN GANNETT

A YEARLING BOOK

Published by Yearling, an imprint of Random House Children's Books
a division of Random House, Inc., New York

Visit us on the Web! www.randomhouse.com/kids

Educators and librarians, for a variety of teaching tools, visit us at
www.randomhouse.com/teachers

ISBN: 0-440-42121-7

Reprinted by arrangement with Random House Books for Young Readers

Printed in the United States of America

January 2006

40 39 38

OPM

For My
FATHER

CONTENTS

Chapter One

MY FATHER MEETS THE CAT

One cold rainy day when my father was a little boy, he met an old alley cat on his street. The cat was very drippy and uncomfortable so my father said, "Wouldn't you like to come home with me?"

This surprised the cat—she had never before met anyone who cared about old alley cats—but she said, "I'd be very much obliged if I could sit by a warm furnace, and perhaps have a saucer of milk."

"We have a very nice furnace to sit by," said my father, "and I'm sure my mother has an extra saucer of milk."

My father and the cat became good friends but my father's mother was very upset about the cat. She hated cats, particularly ugly old alley cats. "Elmer Elevator," she said to my father, "if you think I'm going to give that cat a saucer of milk, you're very wrong. Once you start feeding stray alley cats you might as well expect to feed every stray in town, and I am *not* going to do it!"

This made my father very sad, and he apologized to the cat because his mother had been so rude. He told the cat to stay anyway, and that somehow he would bring her a saucer of milk each day. My father fed the cat for three weeks, but one day his mother found the cat's saucer in the cellar and she was extremely angry. She whipped my father and threw the cat out the door, but later on my father sneaked out and found the cat. Together they went for a walk in the park and tried to think of nice things to talk about. My father said, "When I grow up I'm going to have an airplane. Wouldn't it be wonderful to fly just anywhere you might think of!"

"Would you like to fly very, very much?" asked the cat.

"I certainly would. I'd do anything if I could fly."

"Well," said the cat, "if you'd really like to fly

that much, I think I know of a sort of a way you
might get to fly while you're still a little boy."

"You mean you know where I could get an airplane?"

"Well, not exactly an airplane, but something
even better. As you can see, I'm an old cat now, but

in my younger days I was quite a traveler. My traveling days are over but last spring I took just one more trip and sailed to the Island of Tangerina, stopping at the port of Cranberry. Well, it just so happened that I missed the boat, and while waiting for the next I thought I'd look around a bit. I was particularly interested in a place called Wild Island, which we had passed on our way to Tangerina. Wild Island and Tangerina are joined together by a long string of rocks, but people never go to Wild Island because it's mostly jungle and inhabited by very wild animals. So I decided to go across the rocks and explore it for myself. It certainly is an interesting place, but I saw something there that made me want to weep."

WILD ISLAND

RIVER

Chapter Two

MY FATHER RUNS AWAY

"Wild Island is practically cut in two by a very wide and muddy river," continued the cat. "This river begins near one end of the island and flows into the ocean at the other. Now the animals there are very lazy, and they used to hate having to go all the way around the beginning of this river to get to the other side of the island. It made visiting inconvenient and mail deliveries slow, particularly during the Christmas rush. Crocodiles could have carried passengers and mail across the river, but crocodiles are very moody, and not the least bit dependable,

7

and are always looking for something to eat. They don't care if the animals have to walk around the river, so that's just what the animals did for many years."

"But what does all this have to do with airplanes?" asked my father, who thought the cat was taking an awfully long time to explain.

"Be patient, Elmer," said the cat, and she went on with the story. "One day about four months before I arrived on Wild Island a baby dragon fell from a low-flying cloud onto the bank of the river. He was too young to fly very well, and besides, he had bruised one wing quite badly, so he couldn't get back to his cloud. The animals found him soon afterwards and everybody said, 'Why, this is just exactly what we've needed all these years!' They tied a big rope around his neck and waited for the wing to get well. This was going to end all their crossing-the-river troubles."

"I've never seen a dragon," said my father. "Did you see him? How big is he?"

"Oh, yes, indeed I saw the dragon. In fact, we became great friends," said the cat. "I used to hide in the bushes and talk to him when nobody was around. He's not a very big dragon, about the size of a large black bear, although I imagine he's grown quite a bit since I left. He's got a long tail and yellow and blue stripes. His horn and eyes and the bottoms of his feet are bright red, and he has gold-colored wings."

"Oh, how wonderful!" said my father. "What did the animals do with him when his wing got well?"

"They started training him to carry passengers, and even though he is just a baby dragon, they work him all day and all night too sometimes. They make him carry loads that are much too heavy, and if he complains, they twist his wings and beat him. He's always tied to a stake on a rope just long enough to go across the river. His only friends are the crocodiles, who say 'Hello' to him once a week if they don't forget. Really, he's the most miserable animal I've ever come across. When I left I promised I'd try to help him someday, although I couldn't see how. The rope around his neck is about the biggest, toughest rope you can imagine, with so many knots it would take days to untie them all.

"Anyway, when you were talking about airplanes, you gave me a good idea. Now, I'm quite sure that if you were able to rescue the dragon, which wouldn't be the least bit easy, he'd let you ride him most anywhere, provided you were nice to him, of course. How about trying it?"

"Oh, I'd love to," said my father, and he was so angry at his mother for being rude to the cat that he didn't feel the least bit sad about running away from home for a while.

That very afternoon my father and the cat went down to the docks to see about ships going to the Island of Tangerina. They found out that a ship would be sailing the next week, so right away they started planning for the rescue of the dragon. The cat was a great help in suggesting things for my father to take with him, and she told him everything she knew about Wild Island. Of course, she was too old to go along.

Everything had to be kept very secret, so when they found or bought anything to take on the trip they hid it behind a rock in the park. The night before my father sailed he borrowed his father's knapsack and he and the cat packed everything very carefully. He took chewing gum, two dozen pink lollipops, a package of rubber bands, black rubber boots, a compass, a toothbrush and a tube of tooth paste, six magnifying glasses, a very sharp jackknife, a comb and a hairbrush, seven hair ribbons of different colors, an empty grain bag with a label saying "Cranberry," some clean clothes, and enough food to last my father while he was on the ship. He couldn't live on mice, so he took twenty-five peanut butter and jelly sandwiches and six apples, because that's all the apples he could find in the pantry.

When everything was packed my father and the cat went down to the docks to the ship. A night watchman was on duty, so while the cat made loud queer noises to distract his attention, my father ran over the gangplank onto the ship. He went down into the hold and hid among some bags of wheat. The ship sailed early the next morning.

Chapter Three

MY FATHER FINDS THE ISLAND

My father hid in the hold for six days and nights. Twice he was nearly caught when the ship stopped to take on more cargo. But at last he heard a sailor say that the next port would be Cranberry and that they'd be unloading the wheat there. My father knew that the sailors would send him home if they caught him, so he looked in his knapsack and took out a rubber band and the empty grain bag with the label saying "Cranberry." At the last moment my father got inside the bag, knapsack and all, folded the top of the bag inside, and put the rubber band around the top. He didn't look just exactly like the other bags but it was the best he could do.

Soon the sailors came to unload. They lowered a big net into the hold and began moving the bags of wheat. Suddenly one sailor yelled, "Great Scott! This is the queerest bag of wheat I've ever seen! It's all lumpy-like, but the label says it's to go to Cranberry."

The other sailors looked at the bag too, and my father, who was in the bag, of course, tried even harder to look like a bag of wheat. Then another sailor felt the bag and he just happened to get hold of my father's elbow. "I know what this is," he said. "This is a bag of dried corn on the cob," and he dumped my father into the big net along with the bags of wheat.

This all happened in the late afternoon, so late that the merchant in Cranberry who had ordered the wheat didn't count his bags until the next morning. (He was a very punctual man, and never late for dinner.) The sailors told the captain, and the captain wrote down on a piece of paper, that they had delivered one hundred and sixty bags of wheat and one bag of dried corn on the cob. They left the piece of paper for the merchant and sailed away that evening.

My father heard later that the merchant spent the whole next day counting and recounting the bags and feeling each one trying to find the bag of dried corn on the cob. He never found it because as soon as it was dark my father climbed out of the bag, folded it up and put it back in his knapsack. He walked along the shore to a nice sandy place and lay down to sleep.

My father was very hungry when he woke up the next morning. Just as he was looking to see if he had anything left to eat, something hit him on the head. It was a tangerine. He had been sleeping right under a tree full of big, fat tangerines. And then he remembered that this was the Island of Tangerina. Tangerine trees grew wild everywhere. My father picked as many as he had room for, which was thirty-one, and started off to find Wild Island.

He walked and walked and walked along the shore, looking for the rocks that joined the two islands. He walked all day, and once when he met a fisherman and asked him about Wild Island, the fisherman began to shake and couldn't talk for a long while. It scared him that much, just thinking about it. Finally he said, "Many people have tried to explore Wild Island, but not one has come back alive. We think they were eaten by the wild animals." This didn't bother my father. He kept walking and slept on the beach again that night.

It was beautifully clear the next day, and way down the shore my father could see a long line of rocks leading out into the ocean, and way, way out at the end he could just see a tiny patch of green. He quickly ate seven tangerines and started down the beach.

It was almost dark when he came to the rocks, but there, way out in the ocean, was the patch of green. He sat down and rested a while, remembering that the cat had said, "If you can, go out to the island at night, because then the wild animals won't see you coming along the rocks and you can hide when you get there." So my father picked seven more tangerines, put on his black rubber boots, and waited for dark.

It was a very black night and my father could hardly see the rocks ahead of him. Sometimes they were quite high and sometimes the waves almost covered them, and they were slippery and hard to walk on. Sometimes the rocks were far apart and my father had to get a running start and leap from one to the next.

After a while he began to hear a rumbling noise. It grew louder and louder as he got nearer to the island. At last it seemed as if he was right on top of the noise, and he was. He had jumped from a rock onto the back of a small whale who was fast asleep and cuddled up between two rocks. The whale was snoring and making more noise than a steam shovel, so it never heard my father say, "Oh, I didn't know that was you!" And it never knew my father had jumped on its back by mistake.

For seven hours my father climbed and slipped and leapt from rock to rock, but while it was still dark he finally reached the very last rock and stepped off onto Wild Island.

Chapter Four

MY FATHER FINDS THE RIVER

The jungle began just beyond a narrow strip of beach; thick, dark, damp, scary jungle. My father hardly knew where to go, so he crawled under a wahoo bush to think, and ate eight tangerines. The first thing to do, he decided, was to find the river, because the dragon was tied somewhere along its bank. Then he thought, "If the river flows into the ocean, I ought to be able to find it quite easily if I just walk along the beach far enough." So my father walked until the sun rose and he was quite far from the Ocean Rocks. It was dangerous to stay near them because they might be guarded in the day-time. He found a clump of tall grass and sat down. Then he took off his rubber boots and ate three more tangerines. He could have eaten twelve but he hadn't seen any tangerines on this island and he could not risk running out of something to eat.

My father slept all that day and only woke up late in the afternoon when he heard a funny little voice saying, "Queer, queer, what a dear little dock! I mean, dear, dear, what a queer little rock!" My father saw a tiny paw rubbing itself on his knapsack. He lay very still and the mouse, for it *was* a mouse, hurried away muttering to itself, "I must smell tum-duddy. I mean, I must tell somebody."

My father waited a few minutes and then started down the beach because it was almost dark now, and he was afraid the mouse really would tell somebody. He walked all night and two scary things happened. First, he just had to sneeze, so he did, and somebody close by said, "Is that you, Monkey?" My father said, "Yes." Then the voice said, "You must have something on your back, Monkey," and my father said "Yes," because he did. He had his knapsack on his back. "What do you have on your back, Monkey?" asked the voice.

My father didn't know what to say because what would a monkey have on its back, and how would it sound telling someone about it if it did have something? Just then another voice said, "I bet you're taking your sick grandmother to the doctor's." My father said "Yes" and hurried on. Quite by accident he found out later that he had been talking to a pair of tortoises.

The second thing that happened was that he nearly walked right between two wild boars who were talking in low solemn whispers. When he first saw the dark shapes he thought they were boulders. Just in time he heard one of them say, "There are three signs of a recent invasion. First, fresh

tangerine peels were found under the wahoo bush near the Ocean Rocks. Second, a mouse reported an extraordinary rock some distance from the Ocean Rocks which upon further investigation simply wasn't there. However, more fresh tangerine peels were found in the same spot, which is the third sign of invasion. Since tangerines do not grow on our island, somebody must have brought them across the Ocean Rocks from the other island, which may, or may not, have something to do with the appearance and/or disappearance of the extra-ordinary rock reported by the mouse."

After a long silence the other boar said, "You know, I think we're taking all this too seriously. Those peels probably floated over here all by themselves, and you know how unreliable mice are. Besides, if there had been an invasion, *I* would have seen it!"

"Perhaps you're right," said the first boar. "Shall we retire?" Whereupon they both trundled back into the jungle.

Well, that taught my father a lesson, and after that he saved all his tangerine peels. He walked all night and toward morning came to the river. Then his troubles really began.

Chapter Five

MY FATHER MEETS SOME TIGERS

The river was very wide and muddy, and the jungle was very gloomy and dense. The trees grew close to each other, and what room there was between them was taken up by great high ferns with sticky leaves. My father hated to leave the beach, but he decided to start along the river bank where at least the jungle wasn't quite so thick. He ate three tangerines, making sure to keep all the peels this time, and put on his rubber boots.

My father tried to follow the river bank but it was very swampy, and as he went farther the swamp became deeper. When it was almost as deep as his boot tops he got stuck in the oozy, mucky mud. My father tugged and tugged, and nearly pulled his boots right off, but at last he managed to wade to a drier place. Here the jungle was so thick that he could hardly see where the river was. He unpacked his compass and figured out the direction he should walk in order to stay near the river. But he didn't know that the river made a very sharp curve away from him just a little way beyond, and so as he walked straight ahead he was getting farther and farther away from the river.

It was very hard to walk in the jungle. The sticky leaves of the ferns caught at my father's hair, and he kept tripping over roots and rotten logs. Sometimes the trees were clumped so closely together that he couldn't squeeze between them and had to walk a long way around.

He began to hear whispery noises, but he couldn't see any animals anywhere. The deeper into the jungle he went the surer he was that something was following him, and then he thought he heard whispery noises on both sides of him as well as behind. He tried to run, but he tripped over more roots, and the noises only came nearer. Once or twice he thought he heard something laughing at him.

At last he came out into a clearing and ran right into the middle of it so that he could see anything that might try to attack him. Was he surprised when he looked and saw fourteen green eyes coming out of the jungle all around the clearing, and when the green eyes turned into seven tigers! The tigers walked around him in a big circle, looking hungrier all the time, and then they sat down and began to talk.

"I suppose you thought we didn't know you were trespassing in our jungle!"

Then the next tiger spoke. "I suppose you're going to say you didn't know it was our jungle!"

"Did you know that not one explorer has ever left this island alive?" said the third tiger.

My father thought of the cat and knew this wasn't true. But of course he had too much sense to say so. One doesn't contradict a hungry tiger.

The tigers went on talking in turn. "You're our

first little boy, you know. I'm curious to know if you're especially tender."

"Maybe you think we have regular meal-times, but we don't. We just eat whenever we're feeling hungry," said the fifth tiger.

"And we're very hungry right now. In fact, I can hardly wait," said the sixth.

"I *can't* wait!" said the seventh tiger.

And then all the tigers said together in a loud roar, "Let's begin right now!" and they moved in closer.

My father looked at those seven hungry tigers, and then he had an idea. He quickly opened his knapsack and took out the chewing gum. The cat had told him that tigers were especially fond of chewing gum, which was very scarce on the island. So he threw them each a piece, but they only growled, "As fond as we are of chewing gum, we're sure we'd like you even better!" and they moved so close that he could feel them breathing on his face.

"But this is very special chewing gum," said my father. "If you keep on chewing it long enough it will turn green, and then if you plant it, it will grow more chewing gum, and the sooner you start chewing the sooner you'll have more."

The tigers said, "Why, you don't say! Isn't that fine!" And as each one wanted to be the first to plant the chewing gum, they all unwrapped their pieces and began chewing as hard as they could. Every once in a while one tiger would look into another's mouth and say, "Nope, it's not done yet," until finally they were all so busy looking into each other's mouths to make sure that no one was getting ahead that they forgot all about my father.

Chapter Six

MY FATHER MEETS A RHINOCEROS

My father soon found a trail leading away from the clearing. All sorts of animals might be using it too, but he decided to follow the trail no matter what he met because it might lead to the dragon. He kept a sharp lookout in front and behind and went on.

Just as he was feeling quite safe, he came around a curve right behind the two wild boars. One of them was saying to the other, "Did you know that the tortoises thought they saw Monkey carrying his sick grandmother to the doctor's last night? But

Monkey's grandmother died a week ago, so they must have seen something else. I wonder what it was."

"I told you that there was an invasion afoot," said the other boar, "and I intend to find out what it is. I simply can't stand invasions."

"Nee meither," said a tiny little voice. "I mean, me neither," and my father knew that the mouse was there, too.

"Well," said the first boar, "you search the trail up this way to the dragon. I'll go back down the other way through the big clearing, and we'll send Mouse to watch the Ocean Rocks in case the invasion should decide to go away before we find it."

My father hid behind a mahogany tree just in time, and the first boar walked right past him. My father waited for the other boar to get a head start on him, but he didn't wait very long because he knew that when the first boar saw the tigers chewing gum in the clearing, he'd be even more suspicious.

Soon the trail crossed a little brook and my father, who by this time was very thirsty, stopped to get a drink of water. He still had on his rubber boots, so he waded into a little pool of water and was stooping down when something quite sharp picked him up by the seat of the pants and shook him very hard.

"Don't you know that's my private weeping pool?" said a deep angry voice.

My father couldn't see who was talking because he was hanging in the air right over the pool, but he said, "Oh, no, I'm so sorry. I didn't know that everybody had a private weeping pool."

"Everybody doesn't!" said the angry voice, "but I do because I have such a big thing to weep about, and I drown everybody I find using my weeping pool." With that the animal tossed my father up and down over the water.

"What—is it—that—you—weep about—so much?" asked my father, trying to get his breath, and he thought over all the things he had in his pack.

"Oh, I have many things to weep about, but the biggest thing is the color of my tusk." My father squirmed every which way trying to see the tusk, but it was through the seat of his pants where he couldn't possibly see it. "When I was a young rhinoceros, my tusk was pearly white," said the animal (and then my father knew that he was hanging by the seat of his pants from a rhinoceros' tusk!), "but it has turned a nasty yellow-gray in my old age, and I find it very ugly. You see, everything else about me is ugly, but when I had a beautiful tusk I didn't worry so much about the rest. Now that my tusk is ugly too, I can't sleep nights just thinking about how completely ugly I am, and I weep all the time. But why should I be telling you these things? I caught you using my pool and now I'm going to drown you."

"Oh, wait a minute, Rhinoceros," said my father. "I have some things that will make your tusk all white and beautiful again. Just let me down and I'll give them to you."

The rhinoceros said, "You do? I can hardly believe it! Why, I'm so excited!" He put my father down and danced around in a circle while my father got out the tube of tooth paste and the toothbrush.

"Now," said my father, "just move your tusk a little nearer, please, and I'll show you how to begin." My father wet the brush in the pool, squeezed on a dab of tooth paste, and scrubbed very hard in one tiny spot. Then he told the rhinoceros to wash it off, and when the pool was calm again, he told the rhinoceros to look in the water and see how white the little spot was. It was hard to see in the dim light of the jungle, but sure enough, the spot shone pearly white, just like new. The rhinoceros was so pleased that he grabbed the toothbrush and began scrubbing violently, forgetting all about my father.

Just then my father heard hoofsteps and he jumped behind the rhinoceros. It was the boar coming back from the big clearing where the tigers were chewing gum. The boar looked at the rhinoceros, and at the toothbrush, and at the tube of tooth paste, and then he scratched his ear on a tree. "Tell me, Rhinoceros," he said, "where did you get that fine tube of tooth paste and that toothbrush?"

"Too busy!" said the rhinoceros, and he went on brushing as hard as he could.

The boar sniffed angrily and trotted down the trail toward the dragon, muttering to himself, "Very suspicious—tigers too busy chewing gum,

Rhinoceros too busy brushing his tusk—must get hold of that invasion. Don't like it one bit, not one bit! It's upsetting everybody terribly—wonder what it's doing here, anyway."

Chapter Seven

MY FATHER MEETS A LION

My father waved goodbye to the rhinoceros, who was much too busy to notice, got a drink farther down the brook, and waded back to the trail. He hadn't gone very far when he heard an angry animal roaring, "Ding blast it! I told you not to go blackberrying yesterday. Won't you ever learn? What will your mother say!"

My father crept along and peered into a small clearing just ahead. A lion was prancing about clawing at his mane, which was all snarled and full of blackberry twigs. The more he clawed the worse it became and the madder he grew and the more he yelled at himself, because it was himself he was yelling at all the time.

My father could see that the trail went through the clearing, so he decided to crawl around the edge in the underbrush and not disturb the lion.

He crawled and crawled, and the yelling grew louder and louder. Just as he was about to reach the trail on the other side the yelling suddenly stopped. My father looked around and saw the lion glaring at him. The lion charged and skidded to a stop a few inches away.

"Who are you?" the lion yelled at my father.

"My name is Elmer Elevator."

"Where do you think you are going?"

"I'm going home," said my father.

"That's what you think!" said the lion. "Ordinarily I'd save you for afternoon tea, but I happen to be upset enough and hungry enough to eat you right now." And he picked up my father in his front paws to feel how fat he was.

My father said, "Oh, please, Lion, before you eat me, tell me why you are so particularly upset today."

"It's my mane," said the lion, as he was figuring

how many bites a little boy would make. "You see what a dreadful mess it is, and I don't seem to be able to do anything about it. My mother is coming over on the dragon this afternoon, and if she sees me this way I'm afraid she'll stop my allowance. She can't stand messy manes! But I'm going to eat you now, so it won't make any difference to you."

"Oh, wait a minute," said my father, "and I'll give you just the things you need to make your mane all tidy and beautiful. I have them here in my pack."

"You do?" said the lion. "Well, give them to me, and perhaps I'll save you for afternoon tea after all," and he put my father down on the ground.

My father opened the pack and took out the comb and the brush and the seven hair ribbons of different colors. "Look," he said, "I'll show you what to do on your forelock, where you can watch me. First you brush a while, and then you comb, and then you brush again until all the twigs and snarls are gone. Then you divide it up in three and braid it like this and tie a ribbon around the end."

As my father was doing this, the lion watched very carefully and began to look much happier.

When my father tied on the ribbon he was all
smiles. "Oh, that's wonderful, really wonderful!"
said the lion. "Let me have the comb and brush and
see if I can do it." So my father gave him the comb
and brush and the lion began busily grooming his
mane. As a matter of fact, he was so busy that he
didn't even know when my father left.

Chapter Eight

MY FATHER MEETS A GORILLA

My father was very hungry so he sat down under a baby banyan tree on the side of the trail and ate four tangerines. He wanted to eat eight or ten, but he had only thirteen left and it might be a long time before he could get more. He packed away all the peels and was about to get up when he heard the familiar voices of the boars.

"I wouldn't have believed it if I hadn't seen them with my own eyes, but wait and see for yourself. All the tigers are sitting around chewing gum to beat the band. Old Rhinoceros is so busy brushing his tusk that he doesn't even look around to see who's going by, and they're all so busy they won't even talk to me!"

"Horsefeathers!" said the other boar, now very close to my father. "They'll talk to me! I'm going to get to the bottom of this if it's the last thing I do!"

The voices passed my father and went around a curve, and he hurried on because he knew how much more upset the boars would be when they saw the lion's mane tied up in hair ribbons.

Before long my father came to a crossroads and he stopped to read the signs. Straight ahead an arrow pointed to the Beginning of the River; to the left, the Ocean Rocks; and to the right, to the Dragon Ferry. My father was reading all these signs when he heard pawsteps and ducked behind the signpost. A beautiful lioness paraded past and turned down toward the clearings. Although she could have seen my father if she had bothered to glance at the post, she was much too occupied looking dignified to see anything but the tip of her own nose. It was the lion's mother, of course, and that, thought my father, must mean that the dragon was on this side of the river. He hurried on but it was farther away than he had judged. He finally came to the river bank in the late afternoon and looked all around, but there was no dragon anywhere in sight. He must have gone back to the other side.

My father sat down under the palm tree and was trying to have a good idea when something big and black and hairy jumped out of the tree and landed with a loud crash at his feet.

"Well?" said a huge voice.

"Well what?" said my father, for which he was very sorry when he looked up and discovered he was talking to an enormous and very fierce gorilla.

"Well, explain yourself," said the gorilla. "I'll give you till ten to tell me your name, business, your age, and what's in that pack," and he began counting to ten as fast as he could.

My father didn't even have time to say "Elmer Elevator, explorer" before the gorilla interrupted, "Too slow! I'll twist your arms the way I twist that dragon's wings, and then we'll see if you can't hurry up a bit." He grabbed my father's arms, one in each fist, and was just about to twist them when he suddenly let go and began scratching his chest with both hands.

"Blast those fleas!" he raged. "They won't give you a moment's peace, and the worst of it is that you can't even get a good look at them. Rosie! Rhoda! Rachel! Ruthie! Ruby! Roberta! Come here and get rid of this flea on my chest. It's driving me crazy!"

Six little monkeys tumbled out of the palm tree, dashed to the gorilla, and began combing the hair on his chest.

"Well," said the gorilla, "it's still there!"

"We're looking, we're looking," said the six little monkeys, "but they're awfully hard to see, you know."

"I know," said the gorilla, "but hurry. I've got work to do," and he winked at my father.

"Oh, Gorilla," said my father, "in my knapsack I have six magnifying glasses. They'd be just the thing for hunting fleas." My father unpacked them and gave one to Rosie, one to Rhoda, one to Rachel, one to Ruthie, one to Ruby, and one to Roberta.

"Why, they're miraculous!" said the six little monkeys. "It's easy to see the fleas now, only there are hundreds of them!" And they went on hunting frantically.

A moment later many more monkeys appeared out of a near-by clump of mangroves and began crowding around to get a look at the fleas through the magnifying glasses. They completely surrounded the gorilla, and he could not see my father nor did he remember to twist his arms.

Chapter Nine

MY FATHER MAKES A BRIDGE

My father walked back and forth along the bank trying to think of some way to cross the river. He found a high flagpole with a rope going over to the other side. The rope went through a loop at the top of the pole and then down the pole and around a large crank. A sign on the crank said:

TO SUMMON DRAGON, YANK THE CRANK

REPORT DISORDERLY CONDUCT

TO GORILLA

From what the cat had told my father, he knew that the other end of the rope was tied around the dragon's neck, and he felt sorrier than ever for the poor dragon. If he were on this side, the gorilla would twist his wings until it hurt so much that he'd have to fly to the other side. If he were on the other side, the gorilla would crank the rope until the dragon would either choke to death or fly back to this side. What a life for a baby dragon!

My father knew that if he called to the dragon to come across the river, the gorilla would surely hear him, so he thought about climbing the pole and going across the rope. The pole was very high, and even if he could get to the top without being seen he'd have to go all the way across hand over hand. The river was very muddy, and all sorts of unfriendly things might live in it, but my father could think of no other way to get across. He was about to start up the pole when, despite all the noise the monkeys were making, he heard a loud splash behind him. He looked all around in the water but it was dusk now, and he couldn't see anything there.

"It's me, Crocodile," said a voice to the left. "The water's lovely, and I have such a craving for something sweet. Won't you come in for a swim?"

A pale moon came out from behind the clouds and my father could see where the voice was coming from. The crocodile's head was just peeping out of the water.

"Oh, no thank you," said my father. "I never swim after sundown, but I do have something sweet to offer you. Perhaps you'd like a lollipop, and perhaps you have friends who would like lollipops, too?"

"Lollipops!" said the crocodile. "Why, that is a treat! How about it, boys?"

A whole chorus of voices shouted, "Hurrah! Lollipops!" and my father counted as many as seventeen crocodiles with their heads just peeping out of the water.

"That's fine," said my father as he got out the two dozen pink lollipops and the rubber bands. "I'll stick one here in the bank. Lollipops last longer if you keep them out of the water, you know. Now, one of you can have this one."

The crocodile who had first spoken swam up and tasted it. "Delicious, mighty delicious!" he said.

"Now if you don't mind," said my father, "I'll just walk along your back and fasten another lollipop to the tip of your tail with a rubber band. You don't mind, do you?"

"Oh no, not in the least," said the crocodile.

"Can you get your tail out of the water just a bit?" asked my father.

"Yes, of course," said the crocodile, and he lifted up his tail. Then my father ran along his back and fastened another lollipop with a rubber band.

"Who's next?" said my father, and a second crocodile swam up and began sucking on that lollipop.

"Now, you gentlemen can save a lot of time if you just line up across the river," said my father, "and I'll be along to give you each a lollipop."

So the crocodiles lined up right across the river with their tails in the air, waiting for my father to fasten on the rest of the lollipops. The tail of the seventeenth crocodile just reached the other bank.

Chapter Ten

MY FATHER FINDS THE DRAGON

When my father was crossing the back of the fifteenth crocodile with two more lollipops to go, the noise of the monkeys suddenly stopped, and he could hear a much bigger noise getting louder every second. Then he could hear seven furious tigers and one raging rhinoceros and two seething lions and one ranting gorilla along with countless screeching monkeys, led by two extremely irate wild boars, all yelling, "It's a trick! It's a trick! There's an invasion and it must be after our dragon. Kill it! Kill it!" The whole crowd stampeded down to the bank.

As my father was fixing the seventeenth lollipop for the last crocodile he heard a wild boar scream, "Look, it came this way! It's over there now, see! The crocodiles made a bridge for it," and just as my father leapt onto the other bank one of the wild boars jumped onto the back of the first crocodile. My father didn't have a moment to spare.

By now the dragon realized that my father was coming to rescue him. He ran out of the bushes and jumped up and down yelling, "Here I am! I'm right here! Can you see me? Hurry, the boar is coming over on the crocodiles, too. They're all coming over! Oh, please hurry, hurry!" The noise was simply terrific.

My father ran up to the dragon, and took out his very sharp jackknife. "Steady, old boy, steady. We'll make it. Just stand still," he told the dragon as he began to saw through the big rope.

By this time both boars, all seven tigers, the two lions, the rhinoceros, and the gorilla, along with the countless screeching monkeys, were all on their way across the crocodiles and there was still a lot of rope to cut through.

"Oh, hurry," the dragon kept saying, and my father again told him to stand still.

"If I don't think I can make it," said my father, "we'll fly over to the other side of the river and I can finish cutting the rope there."

Suddenly the screaming grew louder and madder and my father thought the animals must have crossed the river. He looked around, and saw

something which surprised and delighted him. Partly because he had finished his lollipop, and partly because, as I told you before, crocodiles are very moody and not the least bit dependable and are always looking for something to eat, the first crocodile had turned away from the bank and started swimming down the river. The second crocodile hadn't finished yet, so he followed right after the first, still sucking his lollipop. All the rest did the same thing, one right after the other, until they were all swimming away in a line. The two wild boars, the seven tigers, the rhinoceros, the two lions, the gorilla, along with the countless screeching monkeys, were all riding down the middle of the river on the train of crocodiles sucking pink lollipops, and all yelling and screaming and getting their feet wet.

My father and the dragon laughed themselves weak because it was such a silly sight. As soon as they had recovered, my father finished cutting the rope and the dragon raced around in circles and tried to turn a somersault. He was the most excited baby dragon that ever lived. My father was in a hurry to fly away, and when the dragon finally

calmed down a bit my father climbed up onto his back.

"All aboard!" said the dragon. "Where shall we go?"

"We'll spend the night on the beach, and tomorrow we'll start on the long journey home. So, it's off to the shores of Tangerina!" shouted my father as the dragon soared above the dark jungle and the muddy river and all the animals bellowing at them and all the crocodiles licking pink lollipops and grinning wide grins. After all, what did the crocodiles care about a way to cross the river, and what a fine feast they were carrying on their backs!

As my father and the dragon passed over the Ocean Rocks they heard a tiny excited voice scream, "Bum cack! Bum cack! We dreed our nagon! I mean, we need our dragon!"

But my father and the dragon knew that nothing in the world would ever make them go back to Wild Island.

THE END

If you liked this story, read more about

Elmer's exciting adventures!

Elmer's journey continues in . . .

ELMER AND THE DRAGON

Into the evening sky flew Elmer Elevator aboard the gentle baby dragon, leaving Wild Island behind forever. Elmer, who was nine years old, had just rescued the dragon from the ferocious animals who lived on the island. An old alley cat told him how the dragon had been hurt when he fell from a cloud onto the island, and how the wild animals had made him their miserable prisoner. Elmer, feeling sorry for the dragon, and also hoping to fly on his back, had set off to the rescue.

Now the dragon was free, and happy and grateful, and he said, "Elmer, you were wonderful to come all the way to Wild Island just to rescue me. I'll never be able to thank you enough!"

"Oh, that's all right," said Elmer. "Flying on your back makes all my trouble worthwhile."

"Then I'll take you on a trip! Where would you like to go?"

"Everywhere," said Elmer. "The trouble is that I ran away ten days ago to rescue you, and I guess I ought to be getting home."

"Well, at least I can fly you there."

"That would be swell," said Elmer, peering over the dragon's side. "Let's rest tonight down there on Tangerina Island, and start the trip tomorrow."

"Fine," said the dragon, swooping down and landing beneath a tree on the beach of Tangerina.

Elmer slid down and took off his knapsack. "You're beautiful!" he said, admiring the dragon's blue and yellow stripes, his red horn and eyes, his great long tail, and especially his gold-colored wings shining in the faint moonlight.

"It's very kind of you to say so," said the dragon, suddenly feeling very hungry. "What's there to eat around here?"

"Tangerines all over the place!" said Elmer, picking one and peeling it for the dragon.

"Pew! Pew! What a terrible taste!" choked the dragon, spitting out the tangerine as hard as he could.

"What do dragons eat?" asked Elmer.

"I used to enjoy the skunk cabbages and the ostrich ferns on Wild Island, but I don't see any here," said the dragon, looking anxiously up and down the empty beach.

"Maybe you'd like the tangerine peelings?" suggested Elmer.

The dragon closed his eyes and carefully bit off a small corner of a piece of a peel. Then he jumped up yelling, "Why, they're delicious!"

So Elmer and the dragon ate nineteen tangerines, Elmer the insides and the dragon the peels. A chilly wind blew along the beach and the dragon curled his great long tail around the boy to keep him warm. "Good night!" said Elmer, resting his head on his knapsack. "I can't wait for the trip home tomorrow."

Next morning, as the sun edged over the horizon, the dragon rubbed his eyes, stretched his wings, and yawned. "My, but it's good to be free again! By the way, Elmer, where do you live?"

"In Nevergreen City near Evergreen Park on the coast of Popsicornia," mumbled Elmer, who was already awake and eating tangerines.

"I hope you know how to get there," said the dragon.

"Don't you?" asked Elmer.

"No, don't you?" asked the dragon.

"No," said Elmer. "You see, I came here in the bottom of a boat and I couldn't see where I was going."

"The seagulls will know," said the dragon. "They follow ships out to sea."

"I'll go ask one," said Elmer, suddenly remembering that it would be nice to be home for his father's birthday. He walked down to the water where a very old gull was blinking at the morning sun.

"Excuse me," said Elmer, "but did you ever hear of Nevergreen City?"

"Of course," croaked the very old gull. "I lived there before I followed a ship to Tangerina, but I wouldn't dream of going back now."

"That's very interesting," said Elmer, "but would you know how to go if you did want to?"

"Certainly!" answered the old gull, pointing his right wing toward the ocean. "Just fly in exactly that direction until you get there."

Elmer took out his compass and found that this direction was west northwest. "Is it very far?"

"Far? I should say so!"

"Well, thanks a lot," said Elmer.

"I'm kind of worried," said the dragon. "Suppose we never find it?"

"We'll find it, all right," said Elmer, who was a tiny bit worried himself.

The dragon ran along the beach warming up his wings while Elmer packed sixty-nine tangerines, as many as his knapsack would hold. Besides the tangerines, he had in his knapsack all sorts of things left over from the rescue, including seven pink lollipops (which he was saving for an emergency), half a package of rubber bands, three sticks of chewing gum, a very good jackknife, and a burlap bag. Of course, he kept his compass in his pocket where it would be handy, and he wore his black rubber boots.

"Are you ready?" asked Elmer.

"Jump on!" said the dragon.

Elmer clambered onto the dragon's back and took one last look at Tangerina and the blue and white waves skipping in from the cold ocean onto the sandy beach.

Elmer's adventures with the Dragon
conclude in . . .

THE DRAGONS OF BLUELAND

"Tell me more about your family," said Elmer as the dragon flew over the harbor and northward along the coast of Popsicornia. "Do you all look alike?"

"Oh, no. We've all got gold-colored wings and red feet and horns, but my father is blue and my mother is yellow. All my six sisters are green, ranging from yellow-green to blue-green. We boys are all both blue and yellow. I have wide stripes, but two brothers have narrow stripes, one with the stripes going the other way; one has yellow polka dots on blue, and one blue polka dots on yellow; one has a yellow head and body and one leg, with three blue legs and tail; one is speckled blue and yellow like a bird's egg; and the last has patches of blue and yellow."

"How wonderful! You must look like an Easter parade when you're all out together."

"I guess we do," said the dragon, "especially when Father has us doing our exercises. He's a great one for exercises."

"Exercises?" said Elmer.

"You know, standing on your head and somersaults and leapfrog and all that sort of thing. Of course, in the summer we spend most of our time mowing the meadows and tending to the flowers. Each one of us has a special part of Blueland to take care of. I wonder what's become of my piece. I suppose Mother has taken it over. I had the marshy part near the lakeside. That's why I'm so particularly fond of marsh marigolds and skunk cabbages."

"But what about in the wintertime?" asked Elmer, looking down at the line of waves breaking against the rocky shore in the moonlight. "It must be very cold and snowy, and not much fun for exercising."

"Oh, we do our exercises summer and winter. Father sees to that, and of course we have lots of fun sliding down the mountain slopes onto the frozen lake. But the winter is really fun because we sit in a circle in our cave and Father tells us scary stories about knights. It seems there used to be lots of knights who rode about just looking for dragons. They captured and killed most all of us, but a few escaped to Blueland. My father says his grandfather could remember the knights very well, with their heavy coats of armor and lances and swords and helmets."

"Oh, sure. I've read about them in books," said Elmer. "But those dragons were always fierce and about to eat up somebody."

"Nonsense," said the dragon. "That's just what the knights liked to make people believe, so everybody would think they were very brave when they went dragon hunting. Dragons look fierce sometimes, but they're really very gentle. That's why they finally ran away to Blueland. They wanted to be left alone. And now more men have decided to bother us. Goodness knows what they'll do to us this time. If only we get back in time! We can't possibly make it before tomorrow evening. That will make it over two days since I left."

"Oh, we'll save your family all right," said Elmer hopefully. "I can't wait to see them all." He snuggled up against the baby dragon's neck and dreamed of the rescue as they sped through the night toward the mountains of Blueland.

About the Author and the Illustrator

RUTH STILES GANNETT wrote *My Father's Dragon* just a few years after her graduation from Vassar College in 1944. It was an immediate success, becoming a Newbery Honor Book, and was soon followed by two sequels, *Elmer and the Dragon* and *The Dragons of Blueland*. All three dragon stories have been continuously in print in the more than fifty years since their publication. The author's other books include *Katie and the Sad Noise* and *The Wonderful House-Boat-Train*. She was married to Peter Kahn, an artist and calligrapher. They have seven daughters.

RUTH CHRISMAN GANNETT was already a well-established illustrator when she began collaborating with her stepdaughter on *My Father's Dragon* and its sequels. Her pictures for these books are perhaps her most enduring work. Her illustrations can also be seen in the first edition of John Steinbeck's *Tortilla Flat* and in *Miss Hickory* by Carolyn Sherwin Bailey. Ruth Chrisman Gannett was married to Lewis Gannett, daily book critic for the *New York Herald Tribune*. She died in 1979.